Memory Land

a place where love lives on

by Jody West

artworks by Rassouli

STARCHILD
PRESS
A DIVISION OF
LIGHT TECHNOLOGY
PUBLISHING

My friend Lila had an old cat named Grey.

We were all sad when he passed away.

He stopped breathing.

He was very still.

We took his soft body

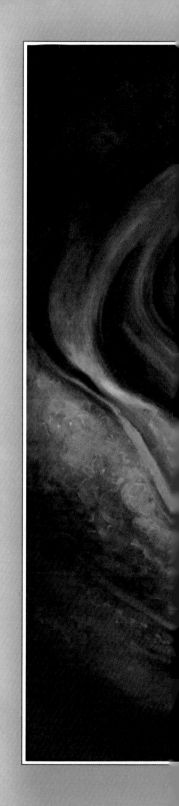

to a **special** place on the hill.

Lila's dad used a shovel

to dig a deep hole.

Grey's body would rest there,

but where was his soul?

Kitties have spirits.

Their memory **remains**

when we see a photo

or remember their **names**.

Even though Grey is gone,

we can think with our hearts

of a place in our imagination

where we are never apart.

Memory Land is like a dream that we see behind our eyes.

We don't have to be sleeping.

We can go there anytime.

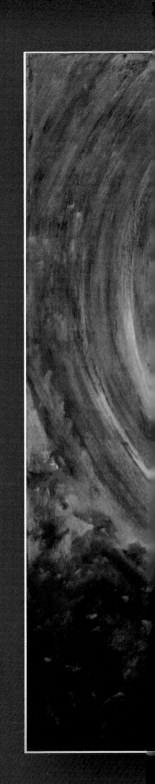

Sometimes we miss my grandma.

She is no longer here.

We talk about her SWEETNESS.

That makes us feel her near.

Grandma is always close,

even though she passed away.

We imagine her in Memory Land

and know that she's okay.

Tears help us remember those who we have loved.

Sometimes we believe they might be up above.

Flying in the heavens,

birds and angels soar.

Does the sky hold our love,

or could there be so much more?

Is Memory Land a place where Spirit runs and plays?

What do they do there,

jump and dance all day?

Memory Land can be

whatever we might dream.

Imagine what makes you happy.

This is what it means.

Envision all the best things:

peace and love and joy,

what everyone wishes

for all girls and boys.

Create that special place

for what we all hold **dear**.

Our loved ones want us to know

there is **nothing to fear**.

Memory Land awaits us all.   It's just a dream away.

Enjoy each moment, and always live for today.

Russell

ISBN-13: 978-1-62233-020-1
Published and printed in
the United States of America by:

STARCHILD
PRESS
A DIVISION OF
LIGHT TECHNOLOGY
PUBLISHING

PO Box 3540
Flagstaff, AZ 86003
800-450-0985 • (928) 526-1345
www.LightTechnology.com

Florida Fusionartist Jody West was inspired to create this story from events
that occurred in her past. Her Grandmother passed away, her friend Jen lost
her life and Grey the cat grew old. Jody's daughter Ellie was only three at
the time, and it was not easy for her to understand all of this. Ellie wanted
answers and decided there is a place where Spirit goes, and she called it
Memory Land. To illustrate the story, Jody photographed the friendship
between Ellie, Lila, and friends. Lila's father, Neal, is the widower of beloved
midwife Jen who tragically passed away while pregnant with Lila. Jen's
loving and passionate spirit will always be remembered. She lives on forever
through her memorial fund at midwiferyschool.org.

Rassouli, a visionary and sage, appeared in the author's hands as a book
cover that was titled *Who Am I? Why Am I Here?*. Immediately discovering
a connection between his artworks and the concept of Ellie's Memory Land,
Jody gave birth to this inspirational story that gives life to the dream of
heaven on Earth.

"Death has nothing to do with going away.
The sun sets.
The moon sets.
But they are not gone."
— Rumi